Parents and Caregivers,

Stone Arch Readers are designed to provide young children reading experiences, as well as opportunities to develop vocabulary, literacy skills, and comprehension. Here are a few ways to support your beginning reader:

- Talk with your child about the ideas addressed in the story.

- Discuss each illustration, mentioning the characters, where they are, and what they are doing.

- Read with expression, pointing to each word. You may want to read the whole story through and then revisit parts of the story to ensure that the meanings of words or phrases are understood.

- Talk about why the character did what he or she did and what your child would do in that situation.

- Help your child connect with characters and events in the story.

Remember, reading with your child should be fun, not forced. Each moment spent reading with your child is a priceless investment in his or her literacy life.

Gail Saunders-Smith, Ph.D.

Stone Arch Readers

are published by Stone Arch Books
a Capstone Imprint
1710 Roe Crest Drive
North Mankato, Minnesota 56003
www.capstonepub.com

Library of Congress Cataloging-in-Publication Data
Yasuda, Anita.
The haunted house / by Anita Yasuda ; illustrated by Steve Harpster.
p. cm. -- (Stone Arch readers: Dino detectives)
Summary: While at the fun park, the Dino detectives decide to visit the haunted house,
but find it a lot more spooky than they expected.
ISBN 978-1-4342-5970-7 (library binding) -- ISBN 978-1-4342-6199-1 (pbk.)
1. Dinosaurs--Juvenile fiction. 2. Haunted houses--Juvenile fiction. 3. Amusement parks--Juvenile fiction.
[1. Dinosaurs--Fiction. 2. Haunted houses--Fiction. 3. Amusement parks--Fiction.
4. Mystery and detective stories.] I. Harpster, Steve, ill. II. Title.
PZ7.Y2124Hau 2013
813.6--dc23   2012046964

Reading Consultants:
Gail Saunders-Smith, Ph.D
Melinda Melton Crow, M.Ed
Laura K. Holland, Media Specialist

Designer: Russell Griesmer

Printed in China by Nordica.
0413/CA21300422
032013
007226NORDF13

The Haunted House

by **Anita Yasuda**
illustrated by **Steve Harpster**

STONE ARCH BOOKS
a capstone imprint

Meet the Dino Detectives!

Dot the Diplodocus

Sara the Triceratops

Cory the Corythosaurus

Ty the T. rex

The Dino Detectives love the
fun park.

They go together every summer.

They go on all the rides. They play all the games.

They eat cotton candy, popcorn, and ice cream.

"Now it's time for the
haunted house," says Cory.

"What haunted house?"
asks Dot.

"That one across the street,"
says Cory.

"That wasn't here last year," says Ty.

"It must be new," says Sara.

A sign on the door says "Do Not Enter."

"Cool," says Cory. "Come on!"

Cory slowly opens the door. It makes a loud creaking sound.

"Why is it so dark?" asks Dot.

"Why is it so dirty?" asks Sara.

"Because it's a haunted house,"
says Cory.

"This is so spooky," says Ty.

Suddenly, a mouse runs over Dot's foot. It runs over Ty's foot, too!

"Ahh!" everyone screams.

Then something flies past Sara's head.

"What was that?" asks Sara.

"It's a ghost!" says Cory. "Let's get out of here!"

The friends run down the dark
hall, screaming the whole way.

A door slowly opens at the end of the hall.

"It's another ghost!" yells Cory.

"I'm not a ghost," a voice says.
"I own this house."

"It's not part of the fun park?"
asks Cory.

"No. I just bought it. I am fixing it up," she says.

"We thought it was a haunted house," says Cory.

"I hope not!" she says.

"Would you like a tour of the house?" she asks.

"Are you sure it's not haunted?"
asks Cory.

"If it is, we can find out together," she said.

"Cool," says Cory. "This is even better than the fun park!"

The other dinos were not sure about that. But they were always up for a new adventure!

STORY WORDS

haunted   spooky   voice

creaking   screaming

Total Word Count: 282